The
MERMAID'S
MUSE

In hopes that you will grow up to see through *your* heart, dear Victoria. — DB
In memory of my grandfather, a celebrated Chinese poet. — Z-YH

First published in 2000 by

RAINCOAST BOOKS
8680 Cambie Street
Vancouver, B.C.
V6P 6M9
(604) 323-7100

www.raincoast.com

1 2 3 4 5 6 7 8 9 10

CANADIAN CATALOGUING IN PUBLICATION DATA

Bouchard, David, 1952-
The mermaid's muse

ISBN 1-55192-248-7

I. Ch'ü, Yüan, ca. 343-ca. 277 B.C.—Juvenile fiction. 2. Dragon boat festival—
Juvenile fiction. I. Huang, Zhong-Yang, 1949- II. Title.
PS8553.O759M47 1999   jC813'.54   C99-910500-0
PZ8.1.B663Me 1999

Printed in Hong Kong

Le Conseil des Arts | The Canada Council
du Canada | for the Arts
DEPUIS 1957 | SINCE 1957

Canada

Raincoast Books gratefully acknowledges the support of the Government of Canada, through the Book Publishing Industry Development Program, the Canada Council and the Department of Canadian Heritage. We also acknowledge the assistance of the Province of British Columbia, through the British Columbia Arts Council.

The MERMAID'S MUSE

the legend of the dragon boats

by DAVID BOUCHARD

paintings by ZHONG-YANG HUANG

RAINCOAST BOOKS

Vancouver

Nay — a better friend I could not find
in all the king's vast holdings,
nor a gentler partner than the one
you have become to me.

And thus it is that I will come with you —
I trust and care for you.
I come not running from this place
but wanting to be near to you.

So it was that early, on a quiet morning, the sea dragon came for Qu Yuan. On this occasion, it arrived in the shape of a spectacular, majestic dragon-shaped boat.

Qu Yuan climbed aboard the boat and together they set out to sea, thinking they would never be seen again.

However, they were seen. They were seen leaving by some villagers.

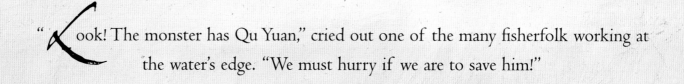

"Look! The monster has Qu Yuan," cried out one of the many fisherfolk working at the water's edge. "We must hurry if we are to save him!"

The villagers had all believed in the sea dragon, though until that time, only one old woman had ever been known to have seen it.

They ran for their boats and paddled out to sea to try to rescue their honored friend. They raced out as quickly as they could, and on any other day would have had no hope of catching up to the dragon. However, on this day, the dragon's head hung low as it listened to the melodious verse of the poet. It did not sense nor care that danger was approaching.